Pony-Crazed Princess

Princess Ellie's Summer Vacation

by Diana Kimpton

Illustrated by Lizzie Finlay

Hyperion Paperbacks for Children
New York

For Cerys and Tegan

First published in the United Kingdom in 2006 as
The Pony-Mad Princess: Princess Ellie's Summer Holiday
by Usborne Publishing Ltd.
Based on an original concept by Anne Finnis
Text copyright © 2006 by Diana Kimpton and Anne Finnis
Illustrations copyright © 2006 by Lizzie Finlay

Printed in the United States of America
First U.S. edition, 2007
1 3 5 7 9 10 8 6 4 2

This book is set in 14.5-point Nadine 2 Normal.

ISBN-13: 978-14231-0616-6
ISBN-10: 1-4231-0616-4

Visit www.hyperionbooksforchildren.com

Chapter 1

"It looks wonderful," yelled Princess Ellie, as she stared out of the helicopter window. She had to shout to be heard above the roar of the engine.

"Fantastic!" agreed her best friend, Kate, at the top of her voice.

They both stared down, watching the tropical island come closer and closer.

Its hills were all covered in thick, green

jungle, and blue sea gently lapped its white, sandy beaches. It looked like the perfect place for a summer vacation. There was only one problem—there was no sign of any ponies.

The helicopter landed gently on a patch of ground marked with an enormous *H*. The wind from its rotor blades sent up clouds of dust that blocked the view from the window. Then the engines finally stopped, and all was quiet.

"Thank goodness," said the Queen. "That trip was too long and too noisy."

"But it was worth it, my dear," said the King. "We've got nothing to do for the next two weeks except relax and swim and make new friends."

"And ride," added Ellie. "You promised there'd be riding." She was starting to worry. If there weren't any ponies, her vacation would be ruined.

Before either of her parents could answer, the helicopter door swung open. "Welcome to Onataki," announced a man in a brightly colored shirt. "Hi! I'm Don—I own the island."

Ellie and Kate followed the King and Queen out of the helicopter. The sun was so bright that it dazzled them. The air was hot, and the gentle breeze carried strange smells that Ellie didn't recognize.

As soon as they were all on the ground, a crowd of smiling women ran forward and hung garlands of flowers around their necks. One of them accidentally knocked the King's crown sideways, but he didn't seem to mind. He just laughed as he pushed it straight.

Kate nudged Ellie with her elbow. "Why aren't they bowing and curtsying like people usually do when they see your parents?"

"Dad says they don't bother with all that here," explained Ellie.

"Lots of the people who come to this island are royal. The others are all millionaires or famous film stars."

"Except me," laughed Kate. Her grandmother was the palace cook.

"And the maids and Higginbottom," added Ellie. She glanced back at the helicopter, where the butler was busy making sure all their luggage was unloaded.

Don led the way to a white building with the word *Reception* written on it in large gold letters. Inside, large palm trees grew in decorative pots, and goldfish swam lazily in a huge pool.

While Don chatted with the King and Queen, the two girls looked around at the walls. There were pictures of people water-skiing and sailing. There were signs about golf and fishing and tennis. But there was nothing at all about horse riding.

Ellie tugged anxiously at her mom's sleeve. "Ask about the ponies," she begged.

"I will in a minute, Aurelia," replied the Queen.

Ellie sighed. She knew from experience that "in a minute" could mean several hours.

Don picked up some keys from the desk. "Come with me, and I'll show you where you're staying." He led the royal group through the reception area and out the other side.

"Wow," cried Kate and Ellie together, as they stepped onto a wide, sun-soaked patio.

Straight in front of them was an enormous swimming pool with water as blue as the sky.

Beyond that lay a wide, sandy beach dotted with striped umbrellas. And on either end of the pool stood the villas for the guests, each with its own garden.

Ellie was glad that their villa was at the far end, closest to the beach. It was totally different from the palace towers she was used to at home. It was much smaller, and it had a shady veranda, with a roof of green tiles. In the garden, hummingbirds flew from flower to flower, and a fountain splashed gently into a shell-shaped pool.

To Ellie's surprise, Higginbottom opened the door to greet them. He was slightly out of breath from rushing to get there before they did, and his garland of flowers looked out of place on top of his evening suit.

He smiled at Ellie and pointed at one of the doors leading off from the sitting room. "That's your room, Your Highness. And Kate's. His Majesty thought you'd like to share."

"Yay!" cried Ellie. She flung the door open and stared in delight at her bedroom. It wasn't pink like her bedroom at home. The tiled floor was creamy yellow, and the covers on the two beds were bright orange.

Kate rushed past her and threw herself

onto the bed nearest the window. "Can I have this one?" she asked. "It's great. I can see the ocean all the time, even when I'm lying down."

"I'm happy with this one," said Ellie, as she bounced up and down on the other bed. Then she spotted an envelope on the dressing table. It had a drawing of a horse at the top, and it was addressed to Princess Aurelia and Kate Brown.

Ellie ripped it open and pulled out a sheet of paper.

The words *Onataki Riding Stables* were written across the top in bright red letters. She danced around the room in excitement as she read the letter.

"Yippee," she yelled. "There really *are* ponies on the island, and Dad's arranged for us to borrow two of them for the entire vacation! We have to go to the stable at nine o'clock tomorrow morning to meet them."

"Super!" cried Kate. "I can hardly wait."

"Neither can I," sighed Ellie. She was already missing her own ponies, even though she'd only said good-bye to them that morning. She looked at the map on the back of the letter and grinned. "Let's go and find the stable now. Surely no one will mind if we just have a quick look."

Chapter 2

"Where are you two going in such a hurry?" asked the Queen, as Ellie and Kate rushed into the garden.

Ellie hesitated. She wasn't sure if her parents would approve of their plans. The letter hadn't said anything about going to the stable that day. "We're . . . um . . ."

". . . Going exploring," finished Kate.

"To find out where everything is," added

Ellie, grateful for her friend's help.

"Good idea," said the King. He leaned back in his lounge chair and sipped from a tall glass decorated with a paper umbrella. "Do you want some lemonade first?"

"Maybe later," said Ellie.

"But not too late," said the Queen, looking at her watch. "We've been invited to a welcome party by the pool, and it starts at five."

"We'll be back by then, I promise," said

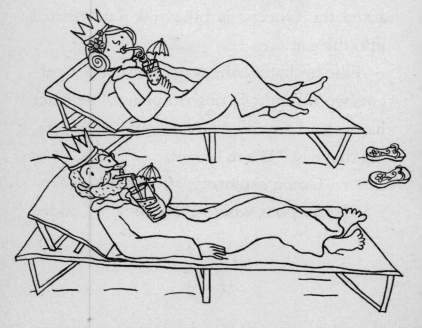

Ellie, as she and Kate ran out of the garden. When they reached the path that ran along the edge of the beach, they stopped and looked at the map.

"Which way is the stable?" asked Kate.

Ellie pointed to the left. "We have to go along here and take the first path that goes inland."

The sun blazed down on them as they walked. It was hot, and the sea looked cool and tempting. But they didn't stop for a splash. They wanted to see the ponies as soon as they could.

They walked on and on. Giant butterflies fluttered past. A lazy lizard sunned itself on a rock. But there was no sign of any inland path. "Did we come the right way?" asked Kate.

"I'm not sure," replied Ellie. "Maybe I had the map upside down." She walked around a clump of palm trees, and there she found the path they'd been looking for. The hoofprints in the sand told her it was the right place.

As they walked along the new path, Kate took a deep breath. "I can smell horses," she squealed. "We must be nearly there."

She was right. A few feet ahead, the path turned sharply and arrived at a row of wooden stalls. A tack room stood at one end, and a muck heap at the other. In front of the stable was a concrete yard, and beyond that was a field surrounded by a wooden fence. All was still and quiet.

"Maybe there's someone in the tack room," suggested Ellie, as she knocked on the door. There was no reply, so she peered inside. Neat racks of saddles hung on the walls, and boxes of grooming supplies sat on the shelves. But there was no sign of anyone.

"Do you think it's all right to look around?" asked Kate.

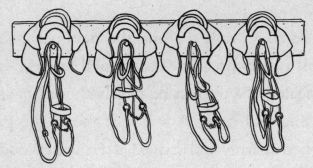

Ellie nodded. "We're not doing any harm," she said. "We're only looking at the ponies."

They walked along the row of stalls, peering over each door in turn. All of the stalls were empty. But each was clean and tidy, with neatly swept floors. Ellie was impressed. The person in charge obviously had high standards.

"The ponies are probably in the field," suggested Kate, running over to the fence.

"I don't think so," said Ellie. The field looked as empty as everywhere else. Then she noticed a large shelter with a roof made of palm leaves on the far side of the field. She shaded her eyes against the sun and peered into it.

It was dark inside, but she could just make out the dim shapes of horses and ponies. "They're in there," she cried. "That's why we couldn't see them from the helicopter."

The girls ran along the fence at the edge of the field until they were as close to the shelter as possible. From there, they could see how cool and shady it looked inside. It was the perfect place for the horses and ponies to doze during the heat of the afternoon.

Ellie climbed onto the bottom bar of the fence and leaned over as far as she could. "Come on," she called.

All the animals raised their heads to see what was happening. The two horses immediately decided that there wasn't anything interesting to see and went back to sleep. But the three ponies wandered out into the sunlight and stared curiously at the two girls.

"I love that skewbald," said Kate, pointing at a cute pony with large brown and white patches on his coat. "He reminds me of Angel."

"But he's a lot bigger," laughed Ellie. Kate's pony, Angel, was only a foal—much too young to ride.

Ellie picked some grass and held it out in the palm of her hand. A light gray pony stepped past the skewbald and walked cautiously toward her. Ellie watched admiringly. He was almost pure white, with a finely shaped head, dainty ears, and a flowing mane. "He's beautiful," she whispered.

"Which is more than can be said for the other one," said Kate.

Ellie giggled as she nodded in agreement. The third pony was the ugliest she had ever seen. His coat was muddy brown, and his head looked slightly too big for his body. Worst of all, he had no mane. Someone had cut it off completely, leaving just a line of stubble along the top of his neck.

Ellie stroked the gray pony as he gently took the grass from her hand. "This one's definitely my favorite," she said. "He's the one I'd like to ride."

"Well, you can't!" said a voice from behind her.

Ellie and Kate spun around to see a girl glowering at them. She had her hands on her hips, a crown on her head, and a scowl on her face.

"That pony is mine!" she yelled.

Chapter 3

Ellie stared in surprise. How could this girl have her own pony on the island when Ellie hadn't been allowed to bring hers? "Is that true?" she asked. "Is the gray pony really yours?"

"Not yet," replied the girl with a smug smile. "But he will be tomorrow. My parents have hired a pony for me for our entire vacation, and I've chosen that one."

"Oh!" said Kate. "We're hiring ponies, too. But we thought the person who runs the stable would decide which ones we would have."

"He probably does, for *ordinary* people," sneered the girl. "But I'm special. I am Princess Clara of Sanbarosa, and I always get my own way."

"You're lucky," said Ellie. "I'm a princess too, but it doesn't work like that for me."

"Perhaps you don't try hard enough," said Clara in a superior voice. Then she turned to stare at Kate. "Are you a princess, too?" she asked.

Kate shook her head. "No, I'm not royal at all."

"How terribly boring for you," said Clara. "And I suppose you don't even have any ponies of your own."

"Yes, I do," replied Kate, firmly. "I've got a gorgeous pony called Angel."

"Only one?" said Clara, looking even more superior. "That's not very impressive. I've got three all to myself."

Ellie stayed quiet. She didn't want to get into a competition with this new girl. But

Kate did. She glared at Clara and announced, "Ellie's got *five* ponies."

Clara's face fell. She obviously wasn't used to being second to anyone. But then she brightened up and announced, "One of my ponies is the best show jumper in all of Sanbarosa. He's won tons of prizes, and he has shelves full of silver trophies. Are any of your ponies champions?"

"No," Kate reluctantly admitted. "Angel's only a foal. She's too young to ride."

"None of mine have ever won anything," said Ellie. She didn't explain that that was hardly surprising. She'd never entered them in any competitions.

Clara smiled smugly again. Then she

glanced at her watch. "Well, I can't waste any more time talking to you," she said. "I have to get changed. I'm going to a fabulous party tonight."

"What a show-off!" said Kate, as they watched Clara run back toward the villas.

"I hope we don't have to ride with her all the time."

"So do I," agreed Ellie.

They gave the gray pony one more handful of grass. Then they said a reluctant goodbye and headed back to their own villa. The sun was lower in the sky now. But it was still hot, and the sea still looked deliciously cool. This time they couldn't resist going in.

They took their sandals off and walked along the water's edge, squealing with delight as the waves rushed over their feet.

Soon they started to run in and out of the water, kicking and splashing until they were both soaked from head to foot. When they finally stopped, they were both very wet and very late.

The King and Queen were already waiting for the girls by the time they got back. "Sorry," said Ellie, as they raced into their villa.

The Queen stared at the two dripping girls. "Never mind," she sighed. "Just get cleaned up and changed into your party clothes as quickly as you can."

By the time Ellie and Kate were ready, the bottom of the shower was covered with sand. Wet footprints led across the bathroom floor to a pile of damp towels that lay abandoned in the bedroom. But both girls looked neat and tidy. Ellie's dress was pink, as usual. Kate's was pale purple, and she had matching ribbons in her hair.

The party was already in full swing when the girls got there with the King and Queen. The steady hum of conversation mingled with the gentle sound of a steel band. Fairy lights glittered in the palm trees. Waitresses carried silver trays of tasty treats, and a wisp of smoke rose from the poolside barbecue.

Don greeted them warmly and led them

toward a group of other guests. "I've got a surprise for you two girls," he said. "There's someone here who is sure to make your vacation even better than you imagined."

Ellie grinned. She loved surprises and couldn't wait to find out who it was. Perhaps it would be a famous movie star. Or, better still, a famous show jumper.

Then Don beckoned to someone in the group. Ellie's excitement quickly turned to dismay, however, when she saw the mystery guest. This wasn't a good surprise at all!

Chapter 4

"This is Princess Clara," said Don.

"A lovely new friend to play with while you're here," added the Queen.

"Oh!" said Ellie, without enthusiasm. "We've already met." She forced herself to smile as she was introduced to Clara's parents, the Duke and Duchess of Sanbarosa. They were both surprisingly pleasant for people with such an awful daughter.

"We're delighted Clara will have friends to play with while she's here," said the Duke. "She doesn't have any at home."

"I'm not surprised," Kate whispered in Ellie's ear.

But Ellie felt a twinge of sympathy. She knew how difficult it was for a princess to make friends. She hadn't had any, either, until Kate came to live at the palace.

Clara went red with embarrassment and glared at her father. "I don't need friends," she declared.

"Don't be silly, dear," said the Duchess, pushing Clara firmly toward Ellie. "Now why don't you three run along and start getting to know each other?"

"That's a splendid idea," said the King. "I'm sure you girls don't want to stay and listen to our boring adult conversations."

The King was right about that. Besides, Ellie knew that there was no point in arguing with her father at the moment. They were stuck with Clara, at least until the end of the party.

Clara had obviously decided the same. "Come on," she ordered. "It's time to eat." She marched off toward the food.

Kate raised her eyebrows. "That girl is so bossy!" she muttered.

"I know," agreed Ellie, as she set off behind Clara. "But she has the right idea. I'm really hungry."

When they reached the barbecue, Clara shoved plates into their hands. "You must have the fish," she announced. "They're an island specialty. They're caught fresh from the sea every day."

Ellie eyed the fish suspiciously. Sure, they smelled delicious as they sizzled over the hot charcoal. But they still had their heads and tails. She wasn't sure she wanted to eat food that seemed to be staring at her. She was also unwilling to follow Clara's orders.

"I'll have the sausages, please," Ellie said, as she held out her plate to the chef.

"And I'll have the veggie kebabs," added Kate.

Clara frowned, but she didn't stop telling the two girls what to do. As soon as they had filled their plates with bread and different salads, she led the way to a table beside the pool. "We'll sit here," she insisted. "We can play Spot the Celebrity while we eat."

Ellie and Kate soon discovered that Clara was much better at that game than they were. She kept pointing out various movie stars, singers, and actors they didn't recognize. The more people she spotted, the more smug she became.

Ellie wished they could stop playing. Seeing famous people was exciting, but

Clara's know-it-all attitude was spoiling the fun. Then Ellie finally noticed someone who looked familiar.

"I'm sure I've seen that tall man somewhere before," she said.

"Of course you have," replied Clara, in her irritatingly superior tone of voice. "That's James Dark. He plays Albert Blonde, secret agent."

"And I think *he* plays the villain," added Kate, pointing excitedly at a small man on the opposite side of the crowd.

Clara looked even more superior. "Don't be silly. He's the lead guitarist from The Willows. Their latest song was number one in Sanbarosa for three whole weeks."

"I've got their CD at home," yelled Kate. "And I still recognized him, even though I thought he was someone else. Does that mean I get a point?"

Before Clara had a chance to reply, a tall, elegant woman walked into the party holding an equally elegant dog on a leash.

"I definitely know him!" cried Ellie. "It's Wilson, the Wonder Dog."

"And Tina Truelove," added Clara, determined not to be outdone. "I love their movies."

"So do I," said Kate. "My favorite's the one where their plane crashes in the mountains and Wilson leads everyone to safety."

"Mine's the one where he saves the little girl from drowning," said Ellie.

"His latest movie is best," declared Clara. "He stops a plot to take over the world, and he rescues a baby from a burning building."

Kate looked puzzled. "I haven't seen that one."

Clara smiled smugly. "Of course you haven't," she explained. "It hasn't been released to ordinary people yet. But *I've* seen an advance copy."

Ellie gritted her teeth and groaned softly. She wished Clara would stop showing off. She really was the most annoying person Ellie had ever met.

Kate stared longingly at Wilson. "He looks so sweet and cuddly. I'd love to pet him."

"Maybe we can," said Ellie. She jumped to her feet and grabbed the last sausage from her plate. "Let's go over and say hello."

"I was just about to suggest that myself," said Clara. She pushed past Ellie and Kate and led the way over to Tina.

When they were only a few steps away, Wilson bounded toward the girls, nearly pulling Tina off her feet. Clara tried to pet him as he rushed past, but he ignored her completely. The only person he was interested in was Ellie.

Tina looked at Ellie with a puzzled expression. "Wow! I've never seen Wilson take to someone so quickly!"

Chapter 5

Ellie smiled shyly. "I think he can smell this," she said, holding out the sausage. Wilson immediately jumped up and whisked it out of her hand. He bit it in two and gulped both pieces down. Then he licked Ellie's hand all over to make sure there was nothing left behind.

"He certainly enjoyed that," laughed Tina. "But don't give him too many. He has to watch his weight for his movies."

Ellie reached down and tickled Wilson's ears. Kate came up beside her and stroked his back. Clara could easily have walked around Ellie to reach the dog. But she didn't. She rudely pushed her way between the two girls and started to pat his head.

Wilson loved all the attention. He licked their faces and wagged his tail so hard that it became a blur. Then he rolled on his back to have his tummy tickled.

"He certainly likes all of you," said Tina. "Do you want to take him for a walk on the beach?"

"Yes, please," said all three girls together. Walking Wilson sounded like lots of fun.

Tina handed the leash to Ellie, who was standing next to her.

Ellie was delighted. She ignored Clara's sulky stare and concentrated on Wilson. He leaped up and down, excited at the prospect of a walk.

"Have fun," said Tina, as the three girls set off. "But be careful not to let him off his leash. He's not used to being on the island,

and I don't want him getting lost."

Ellie felt very proud as she strode across the sand with Wilson bounding along beside her. It felt wonderful to be walking such a beautiful dog in such a beautiful place. He was one of the most famous animals in the whole world, and Tina had trusted *her* to look after him.

Ellie planned to show Wilson the waves. But before they were halfway there, Clara snatched the leash out of her hand. "My turn now," declared the annoying princess. She ran off toward the sea with Ellie and Kate in pursuit.

"Wait for us," yelled Kate, trying her best to catch up.

But Clara didn't wait. Instead she ran even faster. Wilson didn't behave as well for her as he had for Ellie. He tried to race ahead, pulling hard on the leash.

Ellie and Kate caught up with Clara at the edge of the water. Just as they arrived, she bent down and started to fumble with Wilson's neck.

At first, Ellie thought she was just stroking him. Then she realized with horror what Clara was really doing. She was unbuckling the leash.

"Don't do that!" yelled Ellie, grabbing

desperately for Clara's hand. "You'll get us all into trouble."

"Let me go," cried Clara. She wiggled her hand, trying unsuccessfully to free it from Ellie's grasp.

Ellie tightened her grip. "Only if you promise not to let him off his leash," she said.

Clara scowled. "But he's never on a leash in his movies, and he doesn't get lost in those."

Just then, Wilson gave a yelp and jumped backward. His tail wasn't wagging now.

It was tucked firmly between his legs.

Ellie looked around to see what

had frightened him. It was a very small crab scuttling across the sand. The crab couldn't possibly have hurt Wilson, but that didn't stop him from being scared.

"I think Wilson's only acting in his movies," said Ellie, as they stroked the dog to calm him down. "He's not as brave in real life, and he's probably not as clever, either."

"I don't care," said Kate. "He's still really sweet." As if to prove her right, the dog nuzzled her hand and wagged his tail. He was happy again now that the crab was gone.

Clara wasn't. "You might as well have him now," she said, as she thrust the leash into Kate's hand. "Your friend's spoiled all the fun." She turned her back on them and stalked off toward her villa.

Ellie was happy to see her go. The rest of

the evening would be much more enjoyable without her. She just hoped that Clara wouldn't behave that badly when they went riding the next day.

Chapter 6

Breakfast the next morning was very different from what Ellie was used to at home. At the poolside restaurant, Ellie and Kate sat in the shade of a palm tree and ate fresh pineapple, mango, and banana, washed down with coconut milk.

It was so delicious that they were tempted to have second helpings. But there wasn't time. They were determined not to be late for their first vacation ride.

In fact, they were early—and so was Clara. As they arrived, all three ponies looked over their stall doors to see what was happening. The gray pony whickered a welcome. So did the skewbald. But the pony with no mane just shook his head and went back inside.

"I really hope I don't have him," Ellie whispered to Kate. Now that she had seen the gray pony again, she wanted him more than ever.

A short man with a suntanned face came out of the tack room and smiled warmly at the three girls. "Hello," he said. "I'm Simon, the stable groom. And you must be Aurelia, Kate, and Clara."

Clara pulled herself up to her full height

and looked indignant. "That's *Princess* Clara to you," she snapped.

Simon laughed. "Not here," he said. "We don't have formalities like that on this island."

Ellie took an immediate liking to him. "I like to be called Ellie," she said.

"That's fine with me," said Simon. He looked questioningly at Kate.

"Do you prefer to be called something else, too? Bert, maybe, or Esmeralda?"

Kate giggled at the silly suggestion. "My name's fine just as it is."

Simon put down the bucket he

was carrying and looked at the girls carefully. "Now that the introductions are over, I'd better decide which pony each of you will have for the rest of your vacation."

"I want that one," announced Clara, pointing at the gray pony.

Simon shook his head. "It's not a question of who wants what," he explained. "I've got to make sure I match the right rider with the right pony. And that depends on how well you all ride."

Clara put on her superior expression again. "I'm an expert rider," she announced. "I have three ponies of my own at home, and one of them is the best show jumper in Sanbarosa."

Ellie sighed, silently wishing Clara would stop showing off. Then she turned to Simon and said, "I can ride quite well, but I haven't been in any competitions."

"That doesn't matter," said Simon. "Can you walk, trot, and canter?"

"Oh, yes," said Ellie. "And I can jump a little, too."

"So can I," added Kate.

Simon turned to Clara and smiled. "Okay! Since you're the best rider, you can have Mango."

"Is he the gray one?" she asked.

"Oh, no," laughed Simon, as he got the muddy brown pony. "*This* is Mango."

Clara stamped her foot angrily. "I don't want him. He doesn't have a mane."

"That's not his fault," explained Simon, pushing the pony's lead rope into Clara's unwilling hand. "He's very bothered by the flies, because his skin is very sensitive. I clipped off his mane to stop them from getting into it and making him itch."

He ignored Clara's scowl and turned to Kate. "You look as if you'd get along well with Patch. He's the skewbald pony in the stall at this end."

Kate squealed with delight as she went to get him. She'd gotten the pony that she wanted.

Ellie felt excited too. Surely there was only one pony left now—the beautiful gray with whom she'd fallen in love the day before. She crossed her fingers behind her back, hoping there wasn't another pony hidden in one of the other stalls.

To her relief, Simon placed a halter on the gray pony and led him into the yard. "And that leaves you with Cloud," he laughed, as he handed her the rope.

Ellie took it with delight. Cloud was just as beautiful as she remembered. His mane was silky soft, and his coat was as smooth as velvet.

But Clara was furious. "That's not fair!" she yelled. She marched across the yard with Mango and held his rope out to Simon. "I won't ride this horrible pony. I won't, I won't, I won't!"

Simon looked surprised at her outburst. "Calm down," he said. "No one's going to make you ride if you don't want to. Just put Mango in his stall and go back to your parents."

"But I do want to ride," yelled Clara. "I just don't want to ride *him*." She glared at Mango. Then she pointed at Ellie and declared, "I want Cloud, and if I don't get him, I'll cry." She screwed up her face and started to wail loudly.

Ellie could see she was only pretending. The noise sounded realistic enough, but there were no tears to go along with it.

Unfortunately, Simon was more easily fooled. He sighed and led Mango over to Ellie. "I hope you don't mind too much," he muttered, as he took Cloud away. "I didn't realize how much trouble this was going to cause."

Ellie watched miserably as he gave the gray pony to the other princess. It felt worse to have had Cloud and lost him than never to have had him in the first place. Was Clara going to spoil everything on this vacation?

Chapter 7

Ellie felt gloomy as she tied Mango to the fence. He looked so strange without a mane. The place where the mane should have been was hard and bristly. Even worse, the pony didn't seem to like her. He constantly swished his tail and stamped his feet.

"Don't worry about him," said Simon, as he made sure she had tied the quick-release knot properly. "It's the flies he hates, not you."

He checked Kate's and Clara's knots. Then he got boxes of grooming supplies from the tack room and gave one to each of the girls. "I'll look after the ponies when you're not here," he explained. "But when you're at the stable, you'll have more fun if you care for them yourselves."

Once he'd made sure that they knew what all the equipment was for, he left them on their own to groom Mango, Cloud, and Patch, while he looked after his own horse— a chestnut mare called Calypso. "I'm happy to help if you want," he said. "Just call if you need me."

Ellie and Kate were used to grooming. They immediately started to brush their ponies with long, well-practiced strokes. Clara looked less confident. She dabbed so tentatively at Cloud's coat that the brush hardly moved the hairs at all.

Ellie was still upset that Clara had taken Cloud away. But she didn't want that to ruin their vacation, so she tried to be friendly. "You need to brush harder," she suggested. "Stand closer to him and put your weight behind the strokes. Like this—look." She took the brush from Clara's hand and gave a demonstration, sending up a cloud of dust from the pony's coat.

Clara scowled at her and snatched the brush back. "You don't have to show off,"

she complained. "I know perfectly well how to brush a pony. I was just starting gently."

Ellie felt hurt, but she didn't argue. She just went back to concentrating on Mango.

"Don't mind her," whispered Kate. "She's spoiled." But Ellie noticed that Clara did begin to follow her example. Perhaps she had listened after all.

Despite her initial problems, Clara was having a much easier time than Ellie. Cloud stood perfectly still while being groomed. He even lowered his head to let her brush between his ears.

Mango's constant fidgeting made him much harder to groom. Ellie had to be careful not to get stepped on, or hit by his swishing tail. Having no mane to brush saved her some time. But cleaning out his

feet took ages, because he kept putting them down almost as soon as she'd picked them up. As a result, Kate and Clara finished long before she did.

Clara smiled her superior smile again. "I'm so glad I got Cloud," she said. "He's the perfect pony."

Ellie tried to ignore her. It was bad enough that Clara had made her change ponies without having to hear the girl boasting about it.

When Mango was finally ready, Simon checked to make sure that all the saddles and bridles were on properly. Then he made the girls line their ponies up side by side in the yard so he could help each of them mount.

Ellie's stomach churned with nerves as she watched Kate and Clara get on Patch and Cloud. Their ponies stood still for them, but she was sure Mango wouldn't. If he was so difficult to groom, Ellie thought, he was going to be even harder to ride.

When her turn came, Simon walked over and held Mango's bridle. "Cheer up," he said to Ellie. "You'll be fine. There's no need to look so worried."

His words made Ellie feel better. So did the fact that he was making Mango stand still. She picked up his reins, put her foot in the stirrup, and swung herself onto Mango's back. The brown pony flicked his ears back as he felt her weight on his saddle. But, to her relief, he didn't misbehave.

Simon and Calypso led the way out of the yard with Clara and Cloud, while Ellie and Kate followed behind on their ponies. They rode down a path that cut through the middle of a thick jungle.

There were far more flies in the jungle than there had been at the stable, and Mango hated them. He started to toss his large head up and down to keep them away. It worked well, but it made Ellie uncomfortable. It was the first time she had ever ridden a pony that did that, and she didn't know what to do.

She tried shortening the reins. Perhaps that would get him to walk properly. But it didn't. It made him worse. He tossed his head more than ever, fighting the tight pull on his mouth as well as the flies.

Ellie then tried doing the opposite. She let the reins slip through her fingers so they hung long and loose. But that didn't work, either. As soon as Mango felt the pressure removed from his mouth, he knew he was free to do whatever he wanted. And what he wanted to do was eat. He tossed his head once more. Then he swiftly dropped it to the ground and snatched a mouthful of grass.

The sudden movement took Ellie by surprise. She tried to grab his mane to steady herself. But there wasn't any mane. Her fingers closed on empty air.

Chapter 8

Luckily, she didn't fall. But her heart was beating at top speed, and her stomach was knotted with nerves again. She glanced ahead at Clara. At least the other princess wasn't laughing at her. She was too busy enjoying her ride on Cloud to realize that Ellie was having trouble.

Kate was more observant. "Are you all right?" she asked. She waited until Ellie nodded. Then she added, "I wish Mango was as fun to ride as Patch."

"Mango's nicer than you think," said Simon, who had ridden over to see what was wrong. "He just takes a bit of getting used to. Ride up at the front with me, and I'll see if I can help."

Ellie felt more confident beside Simon.

"I don't like it when he tosses his head," she admitted. "I've tried shortening the reins and lengthening them, but nothing seems to work."

Simon smiled. "Hold them just tight enough so you can feel a gentle pressure on his mouth," he explained. "Then move your hands when he tosses his head so you keep that pressure the same all the time. That way you'll always be in control, but you won't jab him in the mouth. Go on, try it."

Ellie listened carefully and tried to do as he said. It was tricky at first, but she soon got used to it. It was much more comfortable for her, and Mango seemed happier, too. He still tossed his head a lot, but at least he seemed more relaxed.

"That's much better," laughed Simon. He looked behind him to see whether Kate and Clara were all right. "Let's try going faster," he called, pushing Calypso into a trot.

Ellie tried to do the same. At first, Mango took no notice and kept walking. Then Ellie pushed harder with her legs, and he finally broke into a bouncy trot, tossing his head in time with his front feet. He wasn't the most comfortable pony she had ever ridden, but at least he was behaving himself for now.

The path brought them to the top of a hill. A large area of short, green grass stretched temptingly ahead of them. Simon urged Calypso into a canter, and Ellie did the same.

She was delighted to find that Mango's canter was much more comfortable than his trot. She smiled happily as she relaxed in the saddle. Deep down inside, she still wished she were riding Cloud. But she was finally starting to enjoy herself. She loved the feel of the wind in her face and the sound of hooves drumming on the ground.

They stopped at the end of the grass and walked slowly to give the ponies a rest. Now that Ellie was used to Mango tossing his head, she could pay more attention to her surroundings. The island was very beautiful

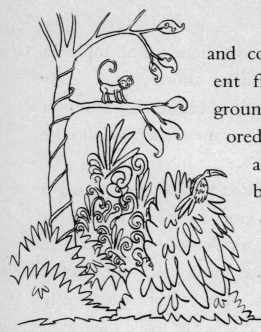

and completely differ-
ent from the palace
grounds. Brightly col-
ored birds squawked
at her from the
bushes, and she
even spotted a
monkey high up
in the branches
of a tree.

Eventually,
Simon led them onto a patch of sand where
someone had built a line of low, wooden
jumps. "I thought it would be fun to finish
the ride with these," he said.

"Great!" said Kate. "I love jumping."

"So do I," said Ellie. She paused and added
in an anxious voice, "But does Mango?"

"Of course he does," replied Simon. "So does Patch. And Cloud is really good at it."

"Oh," said Clara without any enthusiasm. Her face was much whiter than it had been before.

Kate went first and jumped all the fences easily. "Patch is a wonderful jumper," she cried, as she trotted back to the others. "I hope Angel turns out to be as good as he is."

It was Ellie's turn next. She felt a twinge of nerves again, as she rode Mango at a canter toward the first fence. For a moment, she thought he would refuse. But she urged him on,

and he jumped over it easily.

Then he pricked his ears forward and cleared the others without any problems.

"Well done," said Simon. "Now it's Cloud's turn."

Clara gulped, turned even whiter, and cantered the gray pony toward the first fence. Cloud behaved perfectly as he flew over each jump in turn. His rider had more trouble. She lost her right stirrup at the first jump, her left stirrup at the second one, and the reins at the third. By the time she

reached the end, she was clinging to Cloud's neck to keep from falling off.

Simon raced after her. "Are you all right?" he called.

Clara said nothing until Cloud stopped. Then she swiftly put her feet back in her stirrups, sorted out her reins, and sat up straight again. "I'm fine," she insisted, as she trotted over to join the others.

"I don't understand," said Ellie. "You said you'd won lots of show-jumping competitions."

"No, I didn't," snapped Clara. "I said my pony had won them."

"Isn't that the same thing?" asked Kate.

For the first time since they'd met, Clara looked embarrassed. "No," she admitted quietly. "Someone else was riding him."

Ellie was tempted to laugh, but she didn't. She was glad that Kate didn't, either. Clara must have realized that she'd made a fool of herself. There was no need to make her feel even worse.

Chapter 9

Clara avoided Ellie and Kate on the way back. She rode on ahead with Simon, leaving the other two girls to ride together. Ellie liked that arrangement. It felt like riding at home, except that it was much hotter, and they were surrounded by a jungle.

When they reached the stable, they took off the ponies' saddles and bridles, brushed their backs, and turned them loose in the field. Mango, Patch, and Cloud immediately ambled over to the shade of the shelter.

Simon smiled at Kate and Ellie as they hung their saddles in the tack room. "You two ride very well."

"What about me?" asked Clara. "I'm a better rider than either of them."

Ellie stared at her in disbelief. Hadn't she learned anything from her dreadful display of jumping?

"I'm afraid you're not," said Simon. "But don't worry. All three of you ride well enough to take your ponies out without me. There's just one rule. None of you can go riding alone."

"Why not?" asked Kate.

"Because if you're out by yourself, there's no one to call for help if something goes wrong," explained Simon.

"That's not fair," moaned Clara. "They've got each other to ride with, but I'm on my own."

"Don't worry," said Simon. "I can go with you if you don't want to go with Ellie and Kate."

His words seemed to cheer Clara up a little. "I want to ride tomorrow morning," she ordered.

"Sorry," said Simon. "That's the one time I can't manage. Don's asked me to go to some horse sales on the mainland. I won't be back until after dark."

Clara glared at him angrily. As she opened her mouth to argue, Ellie nudged Kate with her elbow. "Let's go," she whispered. "I don't want to see another tantrum."

"Neither do I," said Kate. They ran out of the yard together, leaving Clara arguing with Simon.

When Ellie and Kate got back to the villa, they found Higginbottom getting into the vacation spirit.

He was wearing his black evening suit, as usual. But he had taken off his shoes and socks, rolled up his trousers, and put a straw sun hat on his head.

"The King and Queen have already had lunch and left for the beach," he said. "They hope you'll join them later."

Ellie and Kate changed into T-shirts and shorts and sat down in the shade of the garden. Higginbottom brought them prawn sandwiches and crystal glasses filled with fresh lemonade. While they ate and drank, they made plans.

It was very hot now, and the ponies had already done enough work for the day. So

the girls decided to spend the rest of the afternoon on the beach. Then they would go riding again after breakfast the following day.

"That's when Clara wanted to go," said Kate.

Ellie groaned. "I hope she doesn't ask to go with us. It will be much more fun without her."

As soon as they had finished lunch, they crammed their swimming things into their beach bags and set off to join the King and Queen. But they couldn't resist stopping at the do-it-yourself ice-cream bar on the way.

They each took an empty ice-cream cone. Then they walked along the counter, helping themselves to everything they wanted. Ellie chose strawberry ice cream smothered with maple syrup and chopped nuts.

Kate preferred caramel ice cream topped with chocolate sprinkles. She was just adding a few tiny pieces of fudge when Clara ran up to them.

"Are you riding tomorrow?" she asked, as she grabbed a cone.

"We're going in the morning," said Kate.

"You can come with us if you want," added Ellie, hesitantly. She knew it would be mean not to offer. But she secretly hoped Clara would say no.

"I don't need to," said Clara, as she piled three huge scoops of chocolate ice cream into her cone. "I've just arranged to do something much more exciting after breakfast."

"What is it?" asked Ellie and Kate together.

Clara paused while she drowned her ice cream in strawberry syrup. Then she stuck her nose in the air and smiled her superior smile. "I'm not telling you," she said. "It's a secret."

Chapter 10

Ellie was intrigued. So was Kate. They hung around for a while, hoping Clara would change her mind and tell them the secret. But she didn't. Instead, she glanced scornfully at their bags. "Are you going swimming?" she asked.

"We're going snorkeling, to look at the fish," said Kate, pulling out her snorkel and mask.

"How terribly boring," said Clara. She squirted whipped cream onto her cone so fast that it hit the top and splattered in all directions. "I'm going waterskiing," she announced, completely ignoring the mess. "You can watch me if you like. I'm one of the best water-skiers in Sanbarosa."

"I wonder if she really is," said Kate, as Clara marched off down the beach.

"I don't know," said Ellie, wiping a blob of whipped cream from her nose. "I'm much more interested in what she's planning to do tomorrow. What could possibly be more exciting than riding?"

The two girls wandered across the sand, eating their ice cream as they looked for the King and Queen. They found them relaxing in the shade of a huge, striped umbrella. They had both swapped their heavy royal robes for lightweight cotton ones, and the Queen had a pair of sunglasses perched on her nose.

"I'm glad you're here," said the King. "I need some help with my sand palace." He pointed to an unimpressive heap of sand farther down the beach.

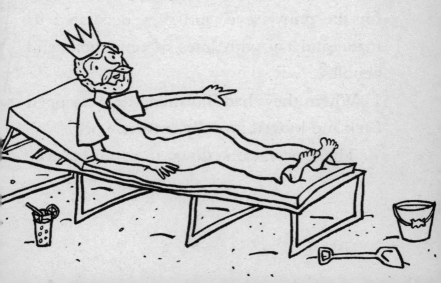

"Does it have to be a palace?" asked Ellie. "A sand pony would be much more fun."

"But it would have to be lying down," pointed out Kate. "Sand legs are much too difficult."

"All right," said the King. "A sand pony it is." He leaped to his feet, picked up a silver bucket and spade, and ran across the beach.

Ellie and Kate followed him and set to work. Soon, they were all laughing and joking as they heaped up the damp sand and patted it into shape. They found a large seashell for the pony's eye, and they decorated its mane and tail with lines of tiny shells and pebbles.

When they had finished, they stepped back and looked proudly at their work.

The Queen came down to admire it, too.

"It's magnificent," she said. "Now I think it's time we all cooled off in the water."

"Splendid idea," said the King. He took off his robe, straightened his ermine-trimmed swimming trunks, and plunged into the water.

The Queen was more cautious. She walked down to the edge of the water and stepped gingerly into the shallow waves. A maid held up the bottom of her robe to keep it from getting wet while she waded.

Ellie and Kate got their snorkels, masks, and flippers, and followed the King into the water. Soon, they were swimming face down across the surface of the sea, looking at the beautiful underwater world beneath them.

Clara was wrong. Snorkeling wasn't boring at all. Ellie had never seen so many different kinds of fish. The smallest flitted about in groups, their scales flashing silver in the sunlight. Between them swam bright blue fish, with long fins like scarves, and red fish with white stripes. Starfish glided silently across the sandy bottom, and a baby turtle swam past them, using its tiny flippers to push itself through the water.

Suddenly, the King tapped Ellie and Kate on the shoulder. "That looks as if it might be fun," he said, as they lifted their faces out of the water.

They stood up and looked where he was pointing. A speedboat was roaring past, towing a small figure on water skis.

"It's Clara," cried Ellie, waving at the other princess. "She really can do it."

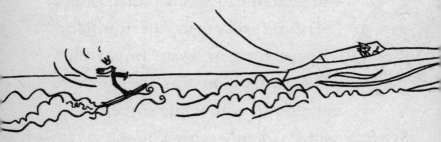

Clara let go of the rope with one hand and waved back, but the movement made her lose her balance. She slipped sideways, fell over, and landed with a splash in the water.

"She's not quite as good as she said," giggled Kate as they watched her being pulled into the boat.

★　★　★

That was the last they saw of Clara that day. They didn't see her at breakfast the next morning, either. And they were so busy looking forward to their ride that they'd forgotten about her secret. As soon as they had finished eating, they set off for the stable. They were almost at the clump of palm trees that hid the path to the stable, when they spotted a familiar figure coming the other way.

"Oh, no," groaned Kate. "It's Clara. I wonder what she's going to show off about this morning."

Ellie couldn't face that superior smile again, and she didn't want to be ordered about anymore. "Quick, let's hide," she cried, as she jumped between two large bushes and pulled Kate in after her.

They crouched behind the leaves, hoping that they wouldn't be discovered. As the other princess came closer and closer, Ellie realized she was crying. And this time the tears were real.

"I wonder what's happened," whispered Kate.

"It must be something awful," Ellie whispered back. Clara didn't look superior or bossy anymore. She just looked utterly miserable. Ellie bit her lip anxiously as she watched her through the bushes. "It's no good," she said. "We've got to do something. I can't bear to see her so upset."

Kate nodded. "Neither can I. Come on!"

They stepped out in front of Clara, trying to look as if there were a good reason that they had been in the bushes. "What happened?" asked Ellie.

Clara stared at them with eyes red from crying. "It's Wilson," she sobbed. "Tina let me take him out for a walk this morning."

"So, that was your secret!" declared Kate.

Clara sniffed loudly and nodded. "I let him off his leash. Tina told me not to, but I thought he'd have more fun if I did. And I was sure he would come back when I called him."

"And did he?" asked Ellie, although she thought she could guess the answer.

"No!" wailed Clara, waving the empty leash in front of their faces. "He ran away so fast that I couldn't keep up with him. Now he's lost, and I'm in big trouble."

Ellie knew what being in big trouble felt like, and she really wanted to help Princess Clara. But Wilson could have been anywhere on the island. How would they ever find him?

Chapter 11

Clara sniffed again and wiped her nose with the back of her hand. "It's no good," she sobbed. "I'll have to tell Tina I've lost Wilson."

"Don't do that yet," said Kate. "Maybe we can find him if we all look together."

Clara shook her head. "He ran away too fast. We'll never catch up with him."

"We might if we take the ponies," said

Ellie. "They can go much faster than he can."

To her surprise, for once the other princess didn't reject her idea. Instead, she gave a half-hearted smile and nodded in agreement.

"I suppose we'd have a chance," Clara admitted.

"That's settled, then," said Kate. "We'll get the ponies ready, while you get your riding hat."

Clara raced off toward her villa. She looked more cheerful now that Ellie and Kate had offered to help. They watched her disappear down the path. Then they turned and ran the other way, heading toward the stable.

They found all three ponies dozing in the thatched-roof shelter. Patch and Cloud came when they called them. Mango was more reluctant to leave the shade. Ellie had to go inside to get him.

There wasn't enough time to groom them properly, so Ellie and Kate quickly brushed their backs. Then they brought the saddles and bridles from the tack room and put them on.

Ellie had just finished fastening Cloud's bridle when Clara ran into the yard, dressed in her riding clothes. "Thanks," she muttered, as she seized hold of the gray pony's reins. "I'll take him now."

Handing over the gray pony reminded Ellie of losing him the day before. But she tried to ignore the twinge of jealousy. At least Clara had said "thanks." That was a huge improvement on her previous behavior. She probably realized that they needed to work together to find Wilson.

As soon as they were all settled on their ponies, the girls trotted out of the yard. Clara went in front, leading them along the route she'd taken with Wilson. Eventually, she stopped in a small clearing surrounded by dense jungle, and she pointed along a path between the trees.

"This is where I last saw him," Clara said. "He ran in there, but I was too out of breath to follow him."

"We'd better hurry," said Kate. "He must be way ahead of us by now."

They pushed the ponies into a canter; their hooves flew across the ground much faster than Wilson could have run. Mango tossed his head as usual, but Ellie was used to that by now. She was even starting to enjoy his bumpy stride, although she still looked enviously at Cloud from time to time.

As they reached the top of a low hill, Clara pulled the gray pony to a halt. "There he is," she cried.

Ellie and Kate rode their ponies up beside her and looked in the direction she was pointing. A long way ahead, Wilson was busy sniffing a bush. His tail was wagging at full speed.

"Wilson!" yelled Clara at the top of her voice. "Come here, boy!"

Wilson stopped sniffing. He looked up and took a step toward the girls. For a moment, Ellie thought he was going to come to them.

Then a small, brown animal shot out of the bushes just in front of him.

It wasn't a rabbit— its ears were much

too short. It looked more like a large guinea pig.

Whatever it was, it didn't seem to like dogs. It took one look at Wilson and ran back into the jungle. The Wonder Dog barked excitedly. Then he hurtled after it and swiftly vanished in the undergrowth.

"Quick! After him!" cried Ellie. She pushed Mango into a gallop and raced off in pursuit. If they didn't hurry, they would lose Wilson again.

Chapter 12

Ellie, Kate, and Clara bent low over their ponies' necks as they galloped down the path. But they had to stop when they reached the place where they had last seen Wilson. They knew he had run into the jungle. But they didn't know which way he'd gone.

"Can you see any tracks?" asked Kate.

Ellie looked around and shook her head.

There were no paw prints, no crushed plants, no dog hairs caught on any twigs—nothing at all to show where Wilson had been.

"We've lost him!" wailed Clara. There was a hint of panic in her voice.

Then they heard an excited bark. "He's over there," shouted Ellie. "It sounds as if he's still chasing that little animal." She turned Mango in the direction of the sound and led the way into the jungle. Clara and Kate followed close behind.

They had to ride slowly now. There was no path, so they had to force their way between the plants and trees. Ellie held her reins in one hand and used the other one to push away the branches.

Each time they heard another bark, they

checked to make sure that they were going in the right direction. But Ellie was worried. Although the ponies could run faster than the dog on open ground, he could wriggle through the jungle more easily than they could. Would they ever manage to catch him?

Suddenly Wilson gave a high-pitched yelp. The sound sent a tingle of fear down Ellie's spine. He didn't sound excited anymore. He sounded scared.

"I hope he's not hurt," said Kate.

"If he is, it's all my fault!" wailed Clara.

Wilson yelped again and again. Ellie was sure he was calling for help. She tried to go faster, but the jungle made that impossible. Mango was already doing the best he could.

They pushed their way between two tall trees and stepped out onto another path. It ran along the edge of a steep, narrow valley, with a fast-flowing river at the bottom. A wooden bridge led from one side to the other, high above the water.

"Which way now?" asked Kate.

As if in answer, Wilson gave a couple

more yelps, followed by a long, plaintive howl. It was the most miserable sound Ellie had ever heard, and it was coming from somewhere across the river.

"He must have gone over the bridge," said Clara.

"We'd better do the same," replied Ellie. She guided Mango toward the bridge. But when the pony reached the edge of the wooden planks, he stopped dead.

"Go on," said Ellie firmly. She squeezed her legs as hard as she could against his sides.

Mango didn't budge. He braced his front legs, refusing to step forward.

"What's wrong with him?" called Kate from the back of the line.

"I don't know," said Ellie. She prodded Mango with her heels. This time the pony moved. But he didn't go forward. He stepped backward and snorted with fear.

"That pony's a pain," grumbled Clara. She started to push past on Cloud. "I bet he's just worried about flies again. You'd better let me go in front."

"No!" cried Ellie. She reached out and grabbed the gray pony's bridle to stop him.

"Let me go!" yelled Clara. "You're not the only one who can lead."

"I know," said Ellie. "But I don't think Mango is being silly. I think he's trying to tell us something, and we should try to figure out what it is." She jumped down from the brown pony's back, keeping hold of his reins. Then she slowly stepped forward onto the bridge.

She put her foot down carefully. The

wood groaned slightly, but it seemed firm enough. She took another step. That was all right, too. But on the third step, the wood splintered under her weight, and her foot plunged downward into empty space.

Ellie screamed as she fell toward the hole. She grabbed for the railing. But it was too far away.

Chapter 13

Ellie's eyes widened in fear as she looked down at the rushing water far below her. She tightened her grip on Mango's reins. It was all she could do to keep from falling. That was when she felt the pony pull back on them. He was helping her to safety. He seemed to realize she was in danger.

Ellie struggled back to the bank and sat down, still shaking with fright.

Kate jumped down from Patch and ran over to her. "Are you all right?" she asked.

"Yes," said Ellie. "Thanks to Mango."

She patted the pony's muddy brown neck and stroked his face.

"Maybe we should go back and get help," said Clara.

Wilson howled again.

"That will take too long," said Ellie. "He sounds like he's in real danger. We need to help him ourselves. . . . If only we could find a way to get across the river."

Kate shuddered. "We can't use that bridge," she said. "It's too dangerous."

"There's no other way to get across," said Clara.

"There might be somewhere to cross farther upstream," suggested Ellie. "Let's ride upriver a little way to check it out. If we don't find anywhere soon, we'll go for help."

They rode off together along the path. Wilson's dismal howls added urgency to their search. The farther they went, the less deep the valley seemed. The sight gave Ellie hope. "Just a little more," she said. "Maybe there'll be a good place to cross soon."

But there wasn't. As they rode around the next bend, they saw a high, rocky cliff straight ahead of them. A huge waterfall tumbled down the cliff into a deep, dark pool that fed the raging river.

"It's beautiful," said Kate, as she stared at the falling water. The sunlight shining through the spray sent a rainbow arching across the cliff.

"Yes, but it's a problem," said Ellie. "We can't go any farther upstream. The cliff is in the way."

"And we still can't cross the river," said Clara. "We have no choice now. We'll have to go back."

"Maybe not," said Ellie, thoughtfully. She vaguely remembered something she'd seen on TV about waterfalls. If the same was true of this one, it might solve their problem. She rode Mango as close as she could to the cliff. Then she crossed her fingers and peered along the rocky wall. To her delight, she saw exactly what she'd hoped to see. Behind the curtain of falling water was a large space. It had been hollowed out by thousands of years of spray from the waterfall.

Ellie beckoned the others over. "It's like a tunnel," she said. "We can walk through it to the other side."

"Are you sure it's safe?" asked Clara.

"I think so," said Ellie. "The floor's flat, and there's plenty of room for the ponies."

They jumped off the ponies and led them toward the tunnel. Ellie went first, with Mango. The brown pony hesitated at the entrance. Then he flicked his ears forward

and followed Ellie onto the wide, rocky ledge. Kate and Clara followed close behind with Patch and Cloud.

It was easy for them to see where they were going. The sun shone through the falling water, making patterns on the rocky wall. But it was much harder to talk. Inside the tunnel, the roar of the waterfall was deafening. It drowned out everything they said.

There was so much spray that it was like walking through a rainstorm. By the time they reached the other side, they were all soaked to the skin.

But they knew they had to hurry. Wilson needed them. So they quickly remounted and galloped back along the river. Soon their wet clothes were steaming in the hot sun. And by the time they reached the bridge, they were almost dry.

Wilson was still howling. The sound seemed to be coming from a steep slope covered with grass and bushes. But there was no sign of the dog.

Kate looked puzzled. "Where is he?" she asked.

"He must be around here somewhere," said Clara.

Ellie felt just as confused. She scratched the back of her neck thoughtfully and stared at the slope. Then she noticed a pile of rocks at the bottom and ran forward to investigate. As she got closer, she saw they were blocking a hole. It looked like the entrance to a burrow.

The howling had stopped now. Wilson was whining pitifully instead. The noise was coming from inside the hole. Ellie could just see the tip of his nose through a gap at the top of the rocks.

The opening was too small for him to wriggle through. And the rocks were too heavy for him to push aside. There was no way Wilson could get out of the hole by himself. He was completely stuck.

Chapter 14

"I don't understand," said Kate. "If he can't get out, how did he get in there in the first place?"

"He must have chased that strange animal into it," suggested Clara.

Kate still looked puzzled. "But he couldn't have. That gap's not big enough."

Ellie bent down and examined the area around the hole. "I don't think it was this small when he got here." She pointed at some fresh marks on the slope. "The rocks used to be up there. Wilson must have knocked them loose when he ran past. They tumbled down and blocked the entrance after he went in."

"Be careful," said Kate. "If any other rocks fall down, you might get hurt."

Ellie looked up carefully. "There aren't any," she said. "It's safe now. All we have to worry about is getting Wilson out."

They set to work with enthusiasm, moving the rocks away as quickly as they could. Clearing the entrance was harder than they expected. The rocks were rough and heavy. Soon their fingers were sore and their arms ached.

They wanted to rest, but they knew that

they couldn't. They had to get the dog out fast. He was becoming more and more upset. If he panicked, he might hurt himself or bring the roof of the burrow tumbling down on top of him.

"Wilson never needs rescuing in his movies," said Clara, as she struggled to move one of the larger boulders. "He's always rescuing other people."

"But this is real life," said Ellie. She grabbed hold of the other side of the boulder, and together they managed to heave it out of the way.

"Poor Wilson," said Kate. "He's not really a Wonder Dog at all."

There was only one rock left now. But it was much larger than the others. It blocked most of the hole all by itself. Wilson could get his nose past it, but there wasn't enough room for the rest of him. The girls had no choice. They had to move the rock in order to set him free.

Clara gave it an experimental tug. "It's really heavy. I can't shift it at all."

"Maybe we can if we all lift together," suggested Kate. But that didn't work, either. This rock was smoother than the others. It was hard to lift it up when they couldn't get a good grip on it.

Ellie bit her lip thoughtfully. Then she had an idea. "We don't have to lift it at all. We only have to slide it forward far enough to let Wilson wriggle past."

She grabbed a branch from the undergrowth and pushed it under one end of the rock. Then she tried to move it away from the entrance. But the branch snapped. So did the next one she tried and the next.

"You might as well give up," sighed Clara. "That's not going to work."

"But digging might," said Kate. "If we dig a hole under the front of the rock, we might be able to roll it forward."

The three girls kneeled down and clawed at the earth with their sore fingers. But the ground was hard and stony. It was impossible to dig a hole in it with their bare hands.

"We need a spade," said Ellie.

"Or a pickax," added Clara.

"Or a rope," said Kate. "If we had a rope, we might be able to pull the rock forward."

Ellie slumped down on the grass to ease her aching back. Everything looked hopeless. They couldn't rescue Wilson without the right equipment. But she hated the idea of giving up when they were that close.

She stared up at the trees and had an idea. "Look at those vines up there," she said excitedly, as she leaped to her feet. "We could use one of those as a rope."

"Brilliant!" said Kate.

"Are you sure they're strong enough?" asked Clara.

"No," said Ellie. "But it's worth a try."

They chose the longest vine they could see and pulled it down from the trees. Then Ellie made a big loop in one end, passed it over the top of the rock, and pulled it tight around the middle.

Wilson started barking loudly again. "Don't worry, Wilson," said Kate. "You'll soon be free."

Ellie, Kate, and Clara took hold of the rope and started to pull. They heaved and tugged until their arms ached. But the rock still didn't budge.

Chapter 15

Clara began to cry again. "It's hopeless," she wailed. "We've tried everything, but nothing works. We can't let Wilson suffer anymore. We've got to go for help."

Behind them, Mango stamped his feet and snorted at the flies. Ellie turned and looked at him. Suddenly, she had an idea. He had saved her from falling when the plank on the bridge broke. Perhaps there was a chance he could help again.

"Don't give up yet," she said. She took the dog leash from Clara and clipped it to one of the metal rings on the front of the brown pony's saddle. Then she slipped the vine through the loop at the other end and tied it so it wouldn't slip out. "Walk back, Mango," she said.

At first, Mango just looked puzzled. Then he seemed to realize what he had to do. He took one step backward, then another. As he gradually walked away, the leash tightened and pulled on the vine. Mango braced himself against the strain and kept going.

"Come on. Let's help him," called Ellie. She grabbed hold of the vine and started to pull. So did Kate and Clara.

The extra help from Mango made all the

difference. The rock finally started to move. Very, very slowly it slid away from the hole. As it did so, the gap between the rock and the edge of the hole grew bigger and bigger.

Wilson yelped with delight and wriggled through. He rushed up to the girls, wagging his tail and jumping up to lick their faces. Clara quickly grabbed hold of his collar to

make sure he didn't run away again.

"We've done it," she squealed. Then she smiled at Ellie and Kate. "I can't thank you enough. I'd never have found him without you."

"Don't worry about it," said Kate. "That's what friends are for."

"Anyway, it's Mango who deserves the real thanks," added Ellie. She stroked the pony's face lovingly. "He was fantastic."

"Now let's get Wilson home," said Kate. "Tina will be wondering where he is."

"I'll walk back to the hotel with him," said Clara. "His leash is too short to hold while I'm riding."

"Oh, that's easy," laughed Ellie. She tied a vine to the end of the leash and handed it to Clara. "Now, let's get going."

"That's a good idea," said Kate. "We've got a long ride ahead."

"And a whole vacation to enjoy," added Ellie. "It's going to be much more fun now that we're all good friends."

Clara started to put her foot in Cloud's stirrup, ready to mount. Then she stopped, took her foot out, and led the gray pony over to Ellie instead. "I'm sorry I was so mean to you yesterday," she said, placing his reins in

Ellie's hands. "And to prove it, I want you to have Cloud."

Ellie looked at the gray pony and ran her fingers through his snow-white mane. He was still as beautiful as she'd first thought, but after the adventure they'd just been through, that didn't seem so important anymore. "No, thanks," she said, as she handed his reins back to Clara. "I'd rather have Mango."

She stroked the brown pony's nose lovingly. "He saved Wilson by moving that rock, he saved me from falling into the river, and he saved all of us from going over that dangerous bridge."

Mango snorted and nuzzled her arm affectionately. Then he shook his head and swished his tail, as if keeping the flies away

were more important than remembering
how helpful he was.

Ellie laughed. Then she threw her arms
around the brown pony's neck and hugged
him. "Wilson may not be a Wonder Dog,"
she said. "But Mango really is a Wonder
Pony."

Here's a sneak peek at the next adventure
of the

Pony-Crazed Princess

in

Princess Ellie
Takes Charge

Princess Ellie Takes Charge

Chapter 1

"That's eighteen for me, seventeen for you," announced Princess Ellie as she wrote the score on the blackboard in the tack room. "I'm winning."

"Only for now," said her best friend, Kate. "I haven't had my turn yet."

"Here's your question, Kate," said Meg, the palace groom. "What's the name of the soft part on the bottom of a horse's foot?"

Kate grinned. "That's an easy one. It's the 'frog.'"

Ellie changed the score. "Okay, eighteen all. We're even now."

Meg peered out of the window. "The rain's stopped, and it's getting late. We'd better make this the last round of the quiz."

"Make it a hard one," said Ellie.

"I'll have to," Meg replied. "You've both gotten all the questions right so far." She paused thoughtfully for a moment. Then she said, "I have one. Suppose you found a pony trying to bite at his stomach and looking around at his sides with a worried expression. What would be the matter?"

"Colic!" cried Ellie.

Meg nodded. "And for a bonus point,

what should you do in that situation?" she asked.

Ellie hesitated. She'd never seen a pony with colic, and she hoped she never would. If she did, she knew she'd ask Meg for help, but that obviously wasn't the answer to the question. "I think I'd call the vet," she suggested.

"That's a good answer," replied Meg. "Colic can be serious—you don't want to take any chances."

Kate updated the score on the board. "You have twenty now," she said. "If I get both parts of my question right, it'll be a tie."

Meg handed her a few small pieces of something sticky. "Do you know what these are?"

Kate stared at the pieces carefully. She

rolled them between her fingers and held them up to her nose to smell them. "Are they oats?" she asked.

"That's right," said Meg. "Now, for that bonus point, can you tell me what you must always do to oats before you put it in a mash for a pony?"

"I know, I know," squealed Ellie. She could hardly resist blurting out the answer.

"Don't tell me!" said Kate. She tapped thoughtfully on her teeth with a fingernail. She stared at her feet and then at the ceiling. Then she stared at the blackboard, as if she hoped the answer would miraculously appear on it. Eventually she admitted, "It's on the tip of my tongue, but I can't remember."

"Don't worry," said Meg. "Let's see if

Ellie really knows the answer."

Ellie felt very pleased with herself. "You have to soak them in hot water for a long time before you feed the mash to ponies."

"Of course," cried Kate. "How could I forget that! If you don't soak the oats, they could clump up and the pony could choke on them."

"Well done, both of you," said Meg. "You're the winner, Ellie. I'm really impressed by how much you've both learned since I came to work at the royal stable."

"That's only because you've taught us tons of stuff about pony care," laughed Ellie. "George never did any of that." George had been the palace groom before Meg. He had lots of rules, most of which began "Princesses don't . . ." and he never allowed

Ellie to help around the stable.

"I'm glad you're here now, Meg," said Kate. "It's so much fun to hang out at the stable when you're around."

"But it won't be much fun if I get in trouble for making you both late," added Meg. "Do you have time to check the ponies' water before you go?"

To find out what happens next, read

Princess Ellie
Takes Charge

Collect all the books in this royally fun pony series!